Too Many DinoSaurs

MERCER MAYER

Holiday House / New York

For Zeb, who also loves monsters

HOLIDAY HOUSE is registered in the U.S. Patent and Trademark Office.

Printed and Bound in May 2011 at Kwong Fat Offset Printing Co., Ltd.,

Dongguan City, China.

The text typeface is Billy Regular.

The artwork was created with simulated pen and ink with watercolor wash

and airbrush, executed in Adobe Photoshop 8.0.

www.holidayhouse.com

First Edition

1 3 5 7 9 10 8 6 4 2

Library of Congress Cataloging-in-Publication Data

Mayer, Mercer, 1943-

Too many dinosaurs / Mercer Mayer. — 1st ed.

p. cm.

Summary: A little boy really wants a dog, but instead he gets dinosaurs!

ISBN 978-0-8234-2316-3 (hardcover)

[1. Dinosaurs—Fiction. 2. Pets—Fiction.] I. Title.

PZ7.M462Tj 2011

[E]—dc22

2010029442

This all started when I asked my mom
if I could have a puppy.
"No," she said. "Now, go outside."

Mr. Jerry was having a yard sale.

Can you guess what I found?

A dinosaur egg!

"Is it real?" I asked.

Mr. Jerry said, "Yes."

So I gave him a dollar
and took it home.

That night I was just about to go
to sleep when I heard a noise.

The egg was cracking.

It was a baby triceratops.

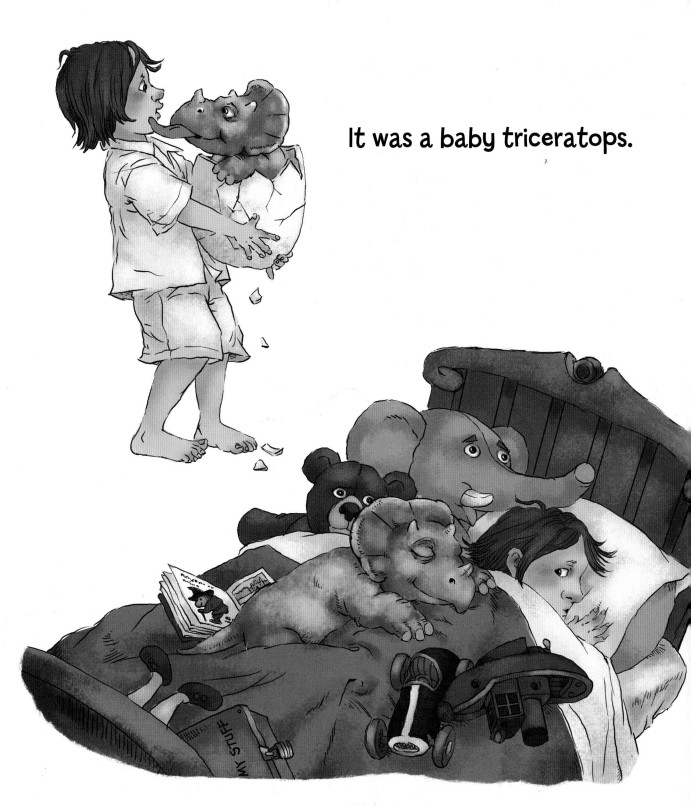

I hoped he'd stay quiet so
Mom wouldn't notice.

The next morning
I heard grunting
outside my window.

The baby dinosaur was ruining Mom's garden.

I ran downstairs, but he was gone;
and there was a hole in our fence.

How would I explain
this to Mom?
Then I heard a scream.

I had a feeling that my dinosaur
had come this way.

Then I found him.

I almost caught up to him when
I ran into Mrs. Littlejohn.

"Why are you running around
in pajamas?" she asked.
"I'm chasing a dinosaur," I said.
"Now go home and put on some clothes," she said.

So I did.

Before I went back out, I gave Mom a big hug. "If I can't have a puppy, can I have a dinosaur?" I asked.

Mom laughed. "If you can find a dinosaur, you may keep it."

Maybe Mr. Jerry would know
how to catch a baby dinosaur.

"What you need is a dinosaur horn," he said.
"It's just a dollar."
Since I didn't have another dollar,
Mr. Jerry let me owe it to him.

At the park I blew the horn
as hard as I could.

The dinosaur horn worked . . .

. . . too well.

"Do something," said Mom.

I blew the horn again.

The dinosaurs began to fade.

Then they were gone.

Mom looked mad.

Mom said, "You need a puppy.
That's it! You're getting a puppy."

That's just what I wanted her to say.

I never saw the baby dinosaur or
the dinosaur horn ever again.

But now I have the best puppy
in the whole world!

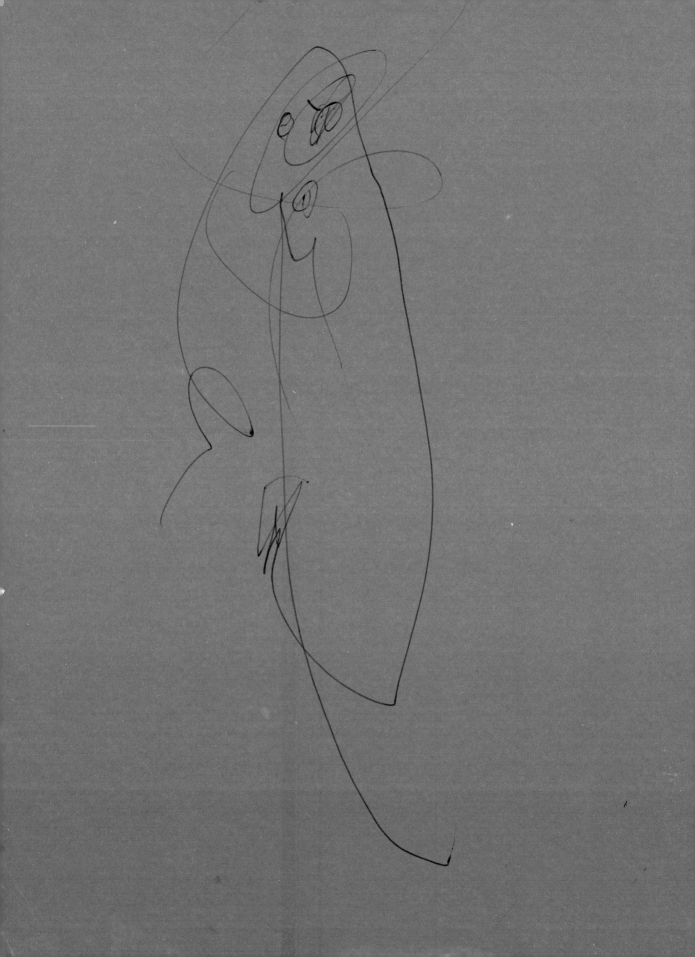